PORTER

The Rescue Dog

Patrick Tame

KeyStroke Publishing

ISBN-9798376646328

Cover design by: Patrick Tame
Library of Congress Control Number: 2018675309
Printed in the United States of America

For Sarah, Henry & Maddie

There is the world that we see and there is the world that we do not see, the world beyond. For reasons I will never fully understand, human nature is to accept things as they first appear and ignore any subsequent evidence to the contrary. In short, the world beyond is not revealed to most people, even when it is in clear sight.

There are a multitude of reasons for this ranging from an evolutionary need to fit in with those around us to sheer laziness of thought. But the real reason most people don't see the world beyond is because most people don't want to see it. Because then they'd have to really *think* and thinking is the very last thing most people want to do. It's much easier if OTHER PEOPLE do the thinking for them and then tell them what to do and by in large this is how how the world works. This is why for the great majority of human history, we believed the world to be flat (which of course it is unless you stand REALLY far away from it) and how small people with big ideas can lead entire nations into terrible danger and destitution.

But there have always been those who walk among us who do look. The people who ask why. The people who don't just accept what other people tell them, the people who ask inconvenient questions. They are the people who sometimes glimpse the world beyond.

The instinct to ask *why* is far stronger amonst children like George and that is why the world of children holds so much more wonder, magic and possiblity than the world of adults. By the time someone reaches adulthood, they have been too worn down and are too busy labouring under the burdon of responsiblity to ever look properly at the world. But for the lucky few, they will always be able to see the world beyond, George is one of these people. That's why his teacher didn't like him and it's precisely why Porter picked him to be his Keeper.

PROLOGUE

The Raven turned it's back to the cold northerly wind as it peered in through a small slit window high up in the tower. He could see a small group of figures stood mournfully around a roaring fire, their hushed voices low as the glow of the flames sent shadows dancing across the stone walls.

The Raven strained to make out a few words amongst the dull murmur but the room fell silent as two robed figures entered the hall flanked by a small dog. The Raven hopped expectantly from one foot to another on his precarious perch.

Inside the chamber, a speech was read, a toast given and the small dog departed alone.

The Raven spread his wings and leapt from his perch, he was tired and hungry and had seen what he had come for.

He was a very old Raven and he had seen it all before.

PORTER

The
Rescue Dog

CHAPTER 1

Mrs Prendercast's Big Idea

It just wasn't fair, George thought to himself as he sat in the back of the car listening to his parents drone on. It wasn't his fault his teacher didn't seem to like him.

They were on their way home from parents evening, George's Dad had met them at school straight from work so they had picked up a take away pizza on the way home. Normally George would be excited at the prospect of a pepperoni pizza but it didn't feel like that tonight.

George looked at the reflection of the street light in the rain running down the window as he munched disinterestedly on a pizza crust, wishing he was somewhere else.

"They didn't say you were doing badly, exactly", chirped his Mum, trying her best to make it sound like she wasn't telling him off. "Just that you don't seem to try hard", she said you had untapped potential and that's actually quite a compliment." The rain drop George was following got to the bottom of the window and he picked another, "If only you applied yourself you could be doing much better".

George's teacher was what his Dad called "Old School". George wasn't entirely sure what Dad meant by this but one thing was for sure, in the eyes of his teacher, George couldn't do anything right.

"I think you're just a bit of a dreamer and maybe Dad's right, she's a bit old school. You only have a term to go so just keep your head down and next year you will have a new teacher and a fresh start".

His Mum seemed to think that a term was nothing but to George, it seemed like a very long time to have to put up with Mrs Gray. Still, at least he had Harry. Harry had been George's best friend since their first week at school when Harry had accidentally taken George's school bag home. Neither of them could stand Mrs Gray and it somehow seemed easier knowing he always had Harry on his side.

"Anyway", continued his Mum in a firm tone of voice that suggested she wanted to move the conversation onto something else, "you've got two weeks of holiday now so lets leave all of that there and just have FUN." George decided his Mum was right. The thought of two whole weeks of no school stretching out in front made him feel lighter and washed over him like a warm bath on a cold day. He was determined to have as much adventure as possible and he decided there and then that this holiday would be the best yet.

Coming in the front door, George headed straight upstairs to his room. The lady from next door, Mrs Prendercast, had been baby sitting Georges little brother Felix and he heard her talking in animated tones to his parents before the front door clicked behind her. As he brushed his teeth and pulled on his pyjamas, he could hear the drone of his parents discussing something in the living room. He couldn't quite make it out but as his parents walked into the hallway he heard his Dad's voice, "Well it's up to you really, you're home more than me but I don't see why not".

"George," called his Mum. "When you have your PJ's on, come downstairs, Dad and I have got something to tell you!"

George had largely forgotten about the parents evening now and was bathing in that Friday night end of term glow kids get when they know they don't have school tomorrow. He bounded down the stairs two at a time, skidded across the floor between his parents who were standing in the hall way and rolled to a stop in the living room, plunging down on his Dads favourite chair. He crossed his arms like a movie villain, furrowed his brow so as to look very serious and said, "Okay, I'm listening". His Dad laughed indulgently and sat down on the sofa whilst his mum stood in the middle of the room and gathered herself for the announcement.

"Well. Now. Dad and I have been talking. You know Mrs Prendercast volunteers at the Dog Rescue in the town? Well, we've been talking to her and your Dad and I have decided that you're old enough now to."

"..TO GET A DOG!!??" George finished her sentence with an exited half exclamation, half question.

"Yes" said his Mum and Dad together.

This was extremely good news. George LOVED animals and had wanted a pet ever since he could remember. He even had dreams that he had a pet dog but his parents had always said that it was never the 'right time', could his wish be about to come true?

There were a number of ways that George might have expected to react to this monumental announcement. Shouting YIPPEE at the top of his voice and running around the living room flapping his arms. Hug his Mum and Dad telling them that they are the best parents ever or possibly just faint. However, in the event, he just sat there, feeling a bit numb. "Seriously?" He uttered quietly, then managed a louder half stammered "Ssseriously?". He felt totally overwhelmed by the emotion.

"Yes", said his Dad firmly, "we're going to get you a pet dog". George's brain finally caught up with his ears, his face broke into a massive smile as tears filled his eyes, he hugged his Mum and Dad at the same time, burying his head slightly in him mum's jumper to hide the tears.

"Tomorrow morning, we're going to go to the pet shop to get all of the things we need, then we're going to go and meet Mrs Prendercast at the Dog Rescue centre to pick one out"

An hour ago, George had thought this was an unequivocally rubbish day, now it was one of the best days possible. He was going to get a dog. A Rescue Dog.

CHAPTER 2

Dog Day

The next morning, George was woken by his brother Felix pulling at his duvet. As he lifted his groggy head from his pillow he remembered that today was Dog Day and vaulted out of bed like coiled spring. The excitement had kept him awake half the night and as a result, George had slept in. He rushed downstairs, wolfed down his breakfast, raced back upstairs and got dressed. As he brushed his teeth he looked out of the window across the garden to his tree house. Yesterday's rain clouds had given way to a clear blue sky, the perfect start to his holiday. He raced back downstairs. "I'm ready to go Dad!", his father looked up from his chair, "Alright, at least let me finish my tea!", George grabbed the car keys, walked out the door and called "Sure, I'll be waiting in the car!" over his shoulder.

Penelope Prendercast was George's very kind, but slightly odd neighbour. She lived alone in Plumb Tree Cottage, a cosy tumbledown house with a thatched roof and a beautifully kept garden. No one knew how old she was but she had lived at

Plumb Tree Cottage along with her cat for longer than anyone in the Village could remember and George had once overheard the retired Colonel telling his Mum that she was older than she looks.

The best thing about Mrs Prendercast was that she was a prolific cake baker. Her kitchen was full of sacks of flower, bags of sugar and jars of all sorts and she could conjure up the most delicious treats; giant chocolate triple cakes, carrot cakes with inch thick frosting, giant choc chip cookies, fruit flans with a dozen different types of fruit, lemon cream buns, chocolate brownies with crunchy and chewy bits, strudels, cheese cakes and even baked alaskas. Every year, Mrs Prendercast ran the cake sale at the annual village fete and people would travel from miles around to queue up for a taste of one of her delicious creations.

She knew the date of every child in the villages birthday and would insist on baking each of them an enormous birthday cake every year, she never forgot anyone. At Christmas she made George's favourite, an enormous sherry trifle which she would bring round to George's house on Boxing Day and insist he have second and third helpings.

Mrs Prendercast was waiting in the car park as they pulled into the Rescue Dog centre, she smiled and gave a little wave. As George stepped out of the car she gave him an appraising look before ushering them through to the kennels.

George was bursting with excitement as Mrs Prendercast explained, "It's really the dog that chooses the person, not the other way around you know" and she gave George just the slightest hint of a wink.

George looked around as they walked through the reception area, it wasn't quite what he had expected. From the outside, it looked like a slightly run down nondescript building with dirty windows and a traffic cone sat in the middle of a pot hole in the car park, but inside it looked different. "This place looks well funded" Muttered Dad quietly as he looked around at the plush interior.

PATRICK TAME

George walked past a large bronze statue of a St Bernard dog next to a little indoor fountain and looked up at the wood panelled walls which were studded with dozens of paintings of dogs. There was a Dog in front of the Great Pyramids, another in front of the Eiffel Tower and one Dog, a poodle, had been painted with a hot air balloon. "Through here" smiled Mrs Prendergast, "They're all very excited to meet you". Through a double doorway was a long large room with a high glass roof. Along each wall were some very comfortable looking dog Kennels with little brass name plates above each one. As George stepped through the door, a scraggly looking terrier with intelligent eyes barked and cocked it's head to one side, looking straight at George. It had patchy fur which was a sort of dirty brown colour and it had ratty teeth. One of his ears was soot black and had been half chewed off, the other was chalky white.

"What's that one called" asked George as he walked towards the kennel, "This is Porter, Porter has been here for quite some time" said Mrs Prendercast with a nervous smile.

"I can see why" said George's Dad, "He looks like he's seen better days. Isn't there something more appropriate?"

"Ah, well now, yes we do have lots of Dogs here but Porter is very discerning and he does seem to have taken a shine to young George here.. He's very choosy you know". Porter barked again as if in agreement. Dad gave Mum a look that seemed to suggest he thought Mrs Predercast had finally lost the plot but Mum shushed him and turned to George.

"He does look very.. well, you know" Mum was trying to be tactful "but I think Dads right, we really should look around a bit more"

George reluctantly followed his parents around the line of kennels peering in at the various dogs, each one looking back with enquiring eyes. There were some magnificent animals, a Great Dane called Captain, a pair of rough strong looking mongrels, one light brown, one reddish dark brown called Scarper and

Scrap, "These two are inseparable" said Mrs P as Mum and Dad briskly moved past, giving their kennel a wide birth. Next was a Dalmatian called Dash, a tiny Jack Russel called Mouse, a Labrador called Skipper who was asleep and lazily opened one eye and half cocked an ear as they ambled past and finally a Chihuahua who sat proudly on top of his kennel looking down at everyone. "Aw, isn't this one cute!" Exclaimed George's mum. The Chihuahua growled slightly at this and Mrs Prendercast ushered them quickly on. George looked at his name plate, it said "Hunter" on it, a funny name for a little dog like that thought George.

"What do you think of the Labrador, or that Dalmatian?" Enquired Georges Dad raising his eyebrows in hope. George walked over to Porters kennel. I think this is the one, said George. "Really?, if you fancy a terrier why not look at this Jack Russel?" But George was transfixed. Porter looked at George, then Porter looked at Mrs Predercast and barked. Mrs Predercast said, "I told you so did I not?", Porter Barked again, "Okay then", she opened the gate and Porter trotted forward, leapt into Georges arms, gave his face an enormous lick and looked over at Georges parents expectantly as if to say, "Come on then, lets go home". Penelope Prendercast looked awkwardly at Georges parents, "As I said, it really is the Dog who chooses the person."

George was bubbling over with a mixture of pride and sheer happiness as they pulled out of the car park with his new best buddy sat on his lap. George's Dad looked up at the sign above the building, "That is strange" he remarked to no one in particular as he drove away, "It says up there, 'Rescue Dogs', surely it should say 'Dog Rescue'". Porter looked up at George, George couldn't be sure, but it looked like Porter winked at him, which was strange, because Dogs can't wink.

CHAPTER 3

Birds on the Roof

A few puffy clouds had formed which gave occasional shady relief from the unseasonably hot sun and George and Porter played together all afternoon in George's garden on the soft grass. "I have to admit, he's quite a dog" remarked Dad as he sipped his afternoon tea and watched Porter leap off of the trampoline and catch a ball mid air for the 5th time in a row. Mrs Predercast had returned from her shift and peered over the low hedge into the garden. "Hello!" She exclaimed, "I see you two are getting along well. Are you having fun?" She asked George. "Yes! Lots, you should see him catch a ball!" Cried George. She then turned directly to Porter and said, "Was I right?". George presumed at first she was aiming this question at his parents but she was looking directly at Porter, and George's mum and dad were out of earshot. Porter gave a crisp Yap, wiggled his ears and wagged his tail before Mrs P bustled off into her kitchen looking satisfied.

As the afternoon drew on, odd things began to happen. Adults spend the majority of their lives looking down. This is because most adults think that they have already seen everything there is to see and believe the world no longer holds any excitement for them, as a result, they stop looking around and look down instead. The problem with this is they are wrong. The world is in fact jam packed full of the most astonishing things that happen all the time but because no one is looking up, they miss it.

George was one of those people who did look up, this was probably why Mrs Gray disliked him so much, she wanted him to stare down at the pages of his text book and memorise endless facts but George was always far more interested in looking up at what was actually happening around him, no text book was ever quite as interesting as the window.

At that moment, George's parents were looking down at their phones, the retired Colonel was looking down at his immaculate grass as he mowed it within an inch of it's life into perfectly straight lines and the man who lived across the street was looking down as he polished the bonnet of his classic car. If any of them had thought to look up at that point, they would have seen what George had seen. An increasingly large collection of birds landing ontop of George's house, so many that his roof looked more like a menagerie than a house.

George gazed around the village at the other roof tops, none of them had so much as a sparrow but George counted 9 birds looking down at him, five ravens, a magpie, a hawk (which George was 90% sure was a Red Kite), two exotic looking lime green parakeets and strangest of all, an Owl. At least a dozen more were circling overhead.

George glanced around and caught site of Mrs P through the hedge in her garden. Her hair was tied up in a bun on top of her head with a ribbon around it and a pen stuck through the middle, she was wearing her jam stained pinny around her waste and had a rolling pin in one hand. Like George, she was staring up at the roof.

"Oh dear" she muttered. "This is bad. Very bad. I didn't think it would happen so soon. I thought we'd have at least a few weeks..

oh well can't be helped." She gazed up for a few seconds more before looking down, catching Georges eye as she did so. "George, you have a lot to learn and time is short. I have a tray of scones about to come out of the oven, you do the eating, I'll do the talking. My house, 5 minutes. Bring Porter."

A few minutes later, George was unlatching the intricate cast iron gate to Plumb Tree Cottage, Porter trotting at his heels. "They aren't quite cool enough yet but they'll have to do, would you like cream and jam?" came the sing song voice from somewhere inside the house. Before he could answer, Mrs P wafted out of the door carrying a tray piled high with scones, an enormous silver spoon topped bowl of double cream and a jar of home made strawberry Jam, the spidery writing on the yellowed label looked like it had been made a very long time ago. Next to the cream was a jug of home made lemonade with large chunks of ice floating in it. She gestured to George to sit down at the garden table, put a bowl of water down on the ground for Porter, which he ignored, and a large bone which he reverently picked up and carried back to George. Porter sat down at Georges feet with the bone taking pride of place between his front paws and looked up, expectantly. Mrs P piled two large current scones onto George's plate, loaded them up with cream and jam and pushed it towards him, "tuck in".

George had heard his Dad say that their neighbour was little eccentric, ten minutes later, George began to think his Dad's assessment was something of an understatement. "The Birds" she began, it always starts with the birds. They see everything and travel fast. They are also the most infernal gossips. Thanks be to goodness that the ones on your roof are all from the this part of the world." She paused and glanced at George, "It means they haven't come from very far away" she added with a conspiratorial look as she noted the confused look on George's cream smeared face. George wasn't following any of this but nodded along with Mrs Prendergast as if this all made perfect sense, after all, Cream Scones were Cream Scones and if the price was listening to a lecture on birds, then so be it.

"The point is, somethings afoot and it's going to happen tonight. If Porter wakes you in the night to go outside, get dressed and go with him. Wherever he goes, stick to him like glue." Mrs Prendercast finally seemed to realise that this was making little sense to George, she patted his hand and absentmindedly dolloped another spoon of cream onto his Scone, "I know this is all going to sound strange at first, but all will become clear my dear". At that moment, his mother called him to come home for dinner. Mrs Prendercast looked up and a strained look came over her normally easy going face, she then spoke very quickly. "Whatever you do, just make sure you are home by sunrise, wear a watch in bed so you know the time. The birds will help. Trust Porter, he knows exactly what to do and if you really get into trouble, send a message with one of the birds." She paused for thought, "It might be an idea to pack a few useful things in a bag to take with you but whatever you do, be home before sunrise." George's mum called his name again, "Have you got it?" "yerffss" said George, spraying crumbs and cream as he tried to say 'yes'. "Good, now, off you go!".

George stood up, brushed the crumbs from his lap, and shouted "COMING" so his mum could hear. He turned back to Mrs Predercast and said, "Thanks for the Scones Mrs P, they are delicious! And I'll be sure to follow Porter, just like you said", and he ran home, Porter scampering along with his enormous bone.

As George lay in bed, he thought about the strange conversation. By dusk, more ravens had arrived in his garden. Space had run out on his roof and they had started perching around his trampoline. The Ravens had then been joined by 5 menacing looking sea gulls, who seemed to have a solemn and serious look as they gazed down their long hook bills. Porter seemed to be completely un-phased by all of this ornithological activity. After dinner, which George had struggled to eat after Mrs P's scones, he had even looked out the window to see Porter sitting happily in the middle of the trampoline, surrounded by the birds as if in deep conversation with them.

What on earth had Mrs P meant? Was she just a rambling old lady or did she really know something?

George didn't think about any of this for long, he yawned as the lack of sleep the previous night combined with the excitement of the day caught up with him and he drifted off into a deep sleep.

CHAPTER 4

Up in the Night

George woke with a start, it was very late but something had roused him from a deep sleep. He rolled over and opened his eyes. There, illuminated by a silver strip of moonlight shining through the gap in his curtains, sat Porter, his wet nose level with George's. Porter began to wag his tail. He nudged George with his nose to make sure he was awake and then padded over to the bottom of the bed, he pulled at the clothes George had been wearing that day from a chair. George rubbed his eyes and swung his legs onto the floor, "Come here boy", Porter returned to nuzzle George's leg for a moment as George ruffled his coarse hair. Porter then went back to the pile of clothes and pulled them across the floor to George and dropped them next to his feet. He sat down looking from the clothes to George and back again, his eyes bright and his tail thumping on the soft carpet. There was no doubt at all as to what Porter wanted. "Okay. Why not" said George softly under his breath. Mrs Predercast had said Porter would want to go out, George wondered why on earth he had to get dressed for the occasion, what was wrong with a dressing gown and slippers? But she had been very clear and Porter was most insistent.

As they slipped quietly down the stairs, George remembered to pick up his watch. Just before opening the door, he glanced around the kitchen. Mrs P's words resonated in his ears and even though he felt very silly, he opened the drawer that his dad kept various useful junk in and picked out a few items. A nearly empty box of matches, a ball of sturdy garden twine, a pocket knife, a half burned birthday cake candle, a small button torch and a packet of short bread biscuits Dad had bought home from a hotel. He jammed them into his pockets and headed to the door. Come on then Porter, I said I'd stick to you like glue.

Up to this point, George hadn't really given much thought as to what might happen next. Had he done so, he would have probably have concluded that Porter liked to go out for a short walk in the night and when all said and done, he could easily just let him run around the garden for a minute or two before letting him back in, job done. But that was very far from what was about to unravel. If George had just the smallest inlking in what would happen once he stepped through that door, he might have thought twice and he might have stuffed more supplies into his pockets too.

He pulled open the door and stood back to let Porter run in front of him, "Come on then boy, lead the way".

Porter bounded purposefully across the garden into the shadow of the sprawling tree that held the treehouse. It seemed to George that there was a slight glow being given off by his dogs ears, more than just the reflected moonlight. Porter paused to check George was behind him before bounding up the ladder. George, noting Porters impressive agility, followed him up.

Later, George would discover that Porter was not like most other dogs. He would discover the reason it said "Rescue Dogs" over the kennels rather than "Dog Rescue" and he would discover the true reason he had been picked out by Porter. But that was later, at this moment in time, all George knew was that he had followed his new pet Dog into his tree house in the middle of the night and he was feeling a bit silly and a bit annoyed not to be in bed, he was also worried what his dad would say if he came into the garden to find him in his treehouse at this time of night. He looked around, this was his treehouse but it looked different somehow. He pulled the small torch out of his pocket and shined it around, it was his treehouse sure enough but he didn't remember it having a door at the *back*. But now he thought about it, had he ever *really looked properly* at the back wall?

Just then, one of the large ravens that had been hanging around the garden earlier in the day flew over to them and settled down on the edge of the Treehouse. "Put that light out dummy" it said in a croak. "Lit up like the Blackpool illuminations". Stunned, George let go of the button and the bright blue light of the torch was replaced again by the soft sliver rays of the full moon.

"Better!" squawked the Rook, "new are ya? Better late than never." Porter let out a low bark and the Rook shuffled closer and looked at George. "Seagulls have warned the Rooks at the Tower, a family of em headed past Graves End, must be turfed back."

George had seen talking birds before but this was different. "What?" he said in astonishment, "what Tower? Who's family? Are you for real?"

"ee's a bit slow this one" said the Raven looking at Porter sympathetically. "Tower of London, Dummy, where d'ya think I've come from? Family of whales av got lost and they're headed up the river Thames. If they get stuckered there when the tide goes out, it's curtins. Can't av that."

"That sounds dreadful Mr.. er, Mr Bird, but what can I possibly do about that?" retorted George politely. Having now overcome the initial shock, he was warming up to the idea of talking Ravens.

"What can you do? Elp im you doughnut" said the Rook, using his beak to gesture to Porter . "Ee's the Rescue Dog in'ee?"

George looked down at Porter, who looked back at him and wagged his tail. His bright eyes positively glowed. "Rescue Dog" he said breathlessly, "Porter, is that what you are? A Rescue Dog?" He said it more loudly this time as the pieces of the jigsaw began to drop into place. "Woof" barked Porter as he jumped at the back door of the tree house, pushed it open and leapt through it to the dark void beyond.

CHAPTER 5

The Treehouse & The Tower

George followed Porter through the small door of the treehouse, the door that had definitely not been there before. As he stepped through he felt his head spinning, a sensation passed through his body, it felt like he had stepped through a waterfall of ice cold jelly. He put his foot down on what appeared to be a stone floor. He looked around, wherever the door led, it was clear he was no longer in a tree and no longer in his garden. Mist hung in the air but he could see the lower part of the sky was lit with the the dim orange glow of a town. Above him he could make out some red lights marking out the tops of high buildings and silhouetted against the black sky were some high castle turrets. He looked back at the door he had come through, it was set in a solid stone wall, through it he could see his tree house and his house beyond, sparkling in the moonlight. As the realisation of what he was looking at hit him, his heart leapt to his mouth and his pulse raced. He took a few deep breaths to calm himself down. "Good grief" he said finally, looking down at Porter who was sitting on the stone flagstones, somehow managing to have each ear pointing in a different direction at the same time.

George weighed his options, the sensible thing would be to go straight back through the door and back to his bedroom, but he discounted that immediately. This was the most exciting thing that had ever happened to him and he had no intention of going home now, and besides, Mrs P had said to stick close to Porter. He thought about Mrs Prendercast for a moment, did she know about this door in his treehouse? There's more to her than meets the eye that's for sure. George barely had time to catch his breath before Porter nudged his leg with his nose and trotted off in the direction of one of the towers. George jogged to catch up.

Through the swirling mist, George worked out that they were on a high walkway of some sort with a drop both sides. Porter lead them into an opening and down a dark stone spiral staircase and out into the fresh air again. As they stepped out, Porter froze, he sniffed the air, his ears pointing dead ahead, one paw poised in mid stride. Porter had sensed something through the mist and soon, George too heard a distinct noise. He pressed himself back into the doorway, ready to run back up the stairs if need be. Clack clack clack, it was a regular snap of smart foot steps getting louder, 'click clack click clack' they seemed to say, then just when George thought that who ever it was making the sound must appear though the darkness, they seemed to turn away. George stepped back out into the mist and followed Porter along the wall moving towards the sound, when all of a sudden he heard a shout "HALT, WHO GOES THERE". In the split second that followed, several things went through George's head. First was fear, he was clearly in trouble and his heart seemed to enter his mouth for the second time that night. Next, he wondered who this person shouting at him was, and how he could see George though the mist that was really quite thick now. Thirdly, he began to really wish had just done the sensible thing and gone back through the door when he had the chance. Then finally, it dawned on him that if he legged it now, he could provably get back into his Garden before anyone could catch him. All of this took a single second but before George could turn this last thought into action, someone else shouted, **"THE KEYS"**. Then followed the most bizarre conversation between two people George had ever heard, it went something like this:

"HALT, WHO GOES THERE"
"THE KEYS"
"WHO'S KEYS"
"THE QUEENS KEYS"
"PASS THE QUEENS KEYS"

Relieved to discover that the shouting hadn't been directed at him, George breathed out, suddenly aware that the tension had caused him to hold his breath. Porter shot forward into the mist, George looked longingly back towards the door which lead back up to the relative safety of his treehouse, then with a shrug, bolted after Porter. He followed him through a very large gateway across some grass towards an imposing building that loomed out of the misty darkness. They came to a stop at the foot of the building where there appeared to be some sort of large wooden scaffolding supporting a ramp up into the building. Porter slid into a gap under the scaffold and George followed him. This was the perfect hiding place, they were totally hidden but they had a good view back across to the gate they had just run though.

A few moments later, they heard the marching feet return, George could see the dark outline of a troop of soldiers with bear skin hats coming through the gate. Recognising them George whispered, "Those are Queens Guards!" under his breath. The gate was shut and the soldiers marched close by the scaffold, George could clearly make out their Grey Coates, rifles and Bear Skin hats. In the Middle of them, one man was dressed differently, George recognised the uniform of a beef eater. "Aha" thought George, "so this must be the Tower of London".

The man in the Beef Eater uniform broke away from the Guardsmen who marched on into the distance and ambled toward the Tower, under which George and Porter were hidden. He pulled a pipe out from somewhere in his person and absentmindedly tapped out the old tobacco and began to re-fill it from a pouch, staring at the moon as he did so.

"Porter" he said quietly without looking down. "I know you're here somewhere. They told me you'd be coming, and with a friend too?". The Beef Eater finally dropped his gaze and looked around, scanning the scene. "Well, I'll go and put the kettle on, you can join me when you've quite finished playing hide and seek" he said gently. With that, he turned on his heel and walked away.

CHAPTER 6

The Raven Master

The Beef Eater was sat in the light of an amber lamp on the doorstep of a little terraced house tucked around out of site, hidden behind the tower just inside the outer walls. He looked different without his smart long jacket and hat but he still had his trousers on, held up over a white vest with a pair of large grey braces. He had a cloth on his lap and a tin of polish on the step next to him and was giving his boots a shine. An unlit pipe poked out of his enormous beard.

Porter wagged his tail excitedly and the man's face lit up as he saw them approach.

"Porter! Good to see you again matey." Porter yapped with delight, the man turned his kindly face to George, "And you must be the new Keeper. I'm not sure I heard properly, but they told me your name was 'Dodge'?"

"It's George" he corrected. "Ah, I see, George, that makes sense. I knew it couldn't be Dodge. They do their best but get the words mixed up a lot you see." George said nothing, he struggled to make conversation with adults at the best of times and right now, he had so many things running around his head, all he could do was just stand there and stare blankly.

The man, sensing Georges befuddlement smiled, stood up and passed him a steaming cup of tea "I put four sugars in it". George, didn't normally drink tea but he appreciated having a hot sweet drink and after a few sips his brain seemed to clear.

"Who told you my name was Dodge?" a Raven landed right on the mans head and sat their looking down at George. "The Ravens. They told me all about you. Where are my manners, allow me to introduce myself, my name is Berwick, or Buster to my friends. I'm the Ravenmaster. Buster bowed as he said this, unseating the Raven who flapped off onto the floor. "Do the ravens talk to you too?" "Oh they talk to me alright, I can't shut them up. They'll talk to anyone but there's not many who actually listen."

It's a little known fact that birds can, and do, talk. Birds, it is now known, are descended from dinosaurs and as such, have had a very, very long time to evolve. They have used this time wisely, birds have conquered every environment from high desert to the deep arctic on both land and water and of course they have they learned to fly (something humans have only managed by cheating). As well as this, they have developed the most intricate and beautiful of languages with as many dialects and variations as there are species of bird. The problem is, most humans can't hear it. This is partly because bird speak is too fast and high pitched for human ears, partly because birds consider humans to be their evolutionary inferiors and so mostly ignore them but it's mainly because most humans KNOW that birds can't talk. Because they KNOW they don't talk, they simply won't listen.

Most people think that the Ravenmaster at the Tower of London was there to feed the Ravens, a sort of Royal Zookeeper. But in fact, the Ravenmaster was very much more than a keeper of birds, he was a keeper of secrets. There had been a Ravenmaster at the Tower of London since before anyone could remember and there had probably been a Ravenmaster on that site for centuries before the Tower was even built. The job passed from Master to Master through the generations and with it, the secrets. The real job of the Ravenmaster was to not to feed the Ravens but to listen to them and keep the King or Queen informed of what was happening in their Kingdom. The Tower had been built on a part of the River that was a major junction for transiting birds and the Ravens picked up all sorts of news during the day. At night, the Ravenmaster sat, drank tea and listened to his Ravens. He would be the first to know about pending danger or other useful titbits like whether the harvest this year was a good one or if there was cold weather coming from the North. He could also find the answer to almost any question, if you asked the birds in the right way. The real skill of the Ravenmaster was to pick out the bits of information that were actually useful or important in amongst the gossip. It's amazing the things that birds give importance too, the Ravens gave equal significance to reports that there were tasty pickings to be had amongst the rubbish behind a certain house in Glasgow as to the fact there was a Spanish Armada sailing to invade England.

With a Raven on each shoulder and another two flapping along overhead, the Ravenmaster lead them towards the river "It's like this, the birds, they can talk to humans right? Well, some humans, but they can't talk to other animals. Porter here, he Understands everything but can't talk to Humans, well, he can make himself understood all right but not with actual language. But he's special, he CAN talk to other animals. I mean, the Ravens say he can talk to ALL of em. That's why the birds go to him sometimes."

George let this sink in. He looked at Porter "Is that true Porter?", "Woof, grr wuff" came the reply.

"He says he can't speak to a Necky Rafts" translated one of the ravens. "Necky rafts?" Said George, "what type of animal are they?"

"You know, Necky Rafts! Big Necks!"

"I think you means Giraffes" corrected The Ravenmaster, he looked across at George, "you get used to it".

They walked down some steps to a sandy bay of shallow water, "Right, this is traitors gate, and here's your boat, just like you asked Porter. Now, the Raven that came to fetch you, Geroff, did he tell you why you was here?".

"He said there were some Whales lost in the Thames?"

"Dead right, your job is to get Porter to them, he'll do the rest. They have already swum past the Tower so you need to head that way" Buster pointed to the right along the river. "The tide is still coming in so it will carry you towards them but it will turn again in about and hour so you should be able to come back again easily enough as it flows back out. They have to get back out before the tide goes fully out or they'll be stuck on the mud. Porter will make them understand."

George and Porter climbed aboard the little wooden boat, it was small but sturdy with a pair of oars and a small outboard engine on the back, "There's a life jacket under the seat, I wouldn't recommend swimming without it, the tide here can be vicious strong." Buster showed George how to start and stop the engine. "Now when you find them, stop the engine, they're scared of the noise and they wont be able to hear a thing with that lump running." He turned to look at one of the Ravens who was now watching proceedings from the top of a wooden post next to the water. "One of you should stay with them, Cumbakeer, how about you?"

The Raven flapped it's wings and hopped obligingly onto the front of the boat with a squawk. "Come on then lazy boots. Let's get a wrinkle on"

"Cumbakeer"? Said George as he fumbled with the engine, I've never heard a name like that before. "That's my Hooman name, it's short for, 'Cumbakeer Withme Sandwich' at your service" he said grandly bobbing his head up and down as if to bow.

Buster smiled at George, "they are very literal when it comes to human names, that's what people tend to say when they see him so as far as he's concerned, that must be his name. It's easiest just to go along with it", he added.

"Are you not coming too?" enquired George, "No." Said Buster firmly. "However much I'd like to, there are rules and we always follow the rules. You're a keeper, your job is to keep Porter here safe. I'm the Ravenmaster, we all have our roles to play and as long as we do, things usually work out right".

With that, Buster pushed the boat with George, Porter and Cumbakeer the Raven out into the flow of the river.

CHAPTER 7

It's Worse Than We Thought..

The little engine chugged away and going with the flow of the tide, they made rapid progress along the River. George was glad to have the life jacket giving his body an extra layer of warmth as the cold wind washed over his face. He steered the boat into the middle of the flow, keeping the river bank insight through the patchy fog.

"That's London Bridge" remarked Cumbakeer as they went under a dark span of steel. He looked across at Porter, "preferred the old one". Porter looked at Cumbakeer and twitched his ears in agreement.

As they emerged onto the other side, George looked back and saw the headlights of a solitary double decker night bus crossing over the top.

Soon they were heading past the looming dome of St Pauls Cathedral, as they approached another bridge, two Gulls swooped low, the tips of their wings glancing off the water. "This will be Blackfriar" said Cumbakeer. "He's pretty big in Gull circles and this bridge belongs to im. Even hoomans calls it 'Blackfriers Bridge'".

Porter barked up at them and they curved around and landed on the side of the boat, nearly knocking one of the oars into the water. "This the new Keeper?" Said one of the gulls to Cumbakeer which George took to be Blackfrier, "Yes. Is name is Dodge" "George" George corrected him, "that's what I said" retorted Cumbakeer brusquely, "Dodge".

"Right". Said Blackfriar. We tried to signal them when they came through, didn't work o course, you'll find them up by the Big Bang". George thought for a moment. Big Bang? He kept going, buildings were rising high on either side of the river and soon he could see the giant wheel of the London Eye on the left side and the Houses of Parliament on the right. Apart from the occasional solitary set of dull headlights briefly crossing a bridge in the distance, London was quiet. Street lamps did their best to illuminate the streets but were no match for the fog which was curling up from the surface of the water and over the river banks on both sides. The only noise was the quiet rumble of George's engine.

The peace was suddenly broken by the sound of Big Ben as it began to strike the hour.
"There it is, The Big Bang". rasped the Blackfriar Gull in satisfaction. George smiled, "You mean Big Ben". "No I don't, it's the Big Bang. Whoever heard of a Ben making a noise like that". George thought about it for a moment and decided there was some logic to this.

He killed the engine and let the boat drift on in the current. Porter stood on the brow of the boat scanning the surface of the water with his ears raised. Then, no more than 50 feet from the boat, a cone like jet of what looked like smoke shot out of the water, Porter leaped from the boat. "Porter!" called George in alarm as the inky black river closed in over the spot where he had entered the water but he was gone. "Calm down" said Cumbakeer, "Leave the flapping to us birds" He and the Blackfriars squawked and cawed together in laughter at this apparent joke. George pulled the small torch out of his pocket and drew it left and right across the water where Porter had jumped, sure enough, he saw Porters head pop up out of the water, making it's way towards what George knew must be one of the whales. He put the torch away and began to row.

George sat in the boat as the three magnificent Whales swam lazily around him in circles, Porter looking very vulnerable and small amongst them. The flow of the tide had now stopped and was beginning to turn so they were drifting neither forward nor backwards and remained stationary outside the Houses of Parliament under the towering Big Ben, or Big Bang as George now thought of it.

The circling went on for some time and at one point one of the magnificent creatures came right next to the boat, lifting it's soulful eye out of the water to have a good look at George.

Finally, Porter swam back to the boat where George helped lift him back on board. Porter shook himself dry, covering everyone in water. Being water birds, the two Gulls didn't seem to mind but Cumbakeer made some angry bird sounds which George could not understand but knew were not polite.

Porter conversed with the birds as George sat quietly. Eventually Cumbakeer looked over at George, "It's worse than we thought. He said. From what these whalleys have told Porter, we have a humbungus problem".

CHAPTER 8

We Need a Faster Boat

Eventually, after working out what a 'ground wobble' meant Cumbakeer managed to relay to George what the family of whales had told Porter.

A large earthquake was about to go off right under the North Sea. Whales are highly sensitive to the slightest noise or vibration and they could feel it coming. Along with half the fish in the North Sea, they were trying to head for the deep water of the Atlantic Ocean as fast at they could but the constant earth tremors had messed up their echolocation and navigation senses and they had got lost in the Thames Estuary.

"Trouble is" Cumbakeer continued, "ee said there's about 100 more of them heading this way""100?!" Exclaimed George. "Yep. She can hear 'em". George looked up the river, his stomach churned and his face flushed hot has he imagined the dreadful scene of 100 whales getting stranded as the tide went out. "We have to stop them! You said that she can hear them, can't she call to them and tell them to turn around?". "Already tried. They can't hear. Too shallow here, too many of them making too much noise. But that's not even the worst of it.". George looked at Cumbakeer and Porter in astonishment, "there's more?" Porter looked down at his paws as Cumbakeer continued on, "She said that the ground wobble will send such a big hello of water down the river that half London will be flooded. She said we have no time to spare"

George thought for a second, a 'Big Hello' of water, he was getting it now, the Raven meant a big wave of water. The earthquake was going to cause a massive wave to flood London!

George now had three problems to solve. Firstly, he needed to lead the family of exhausted Pilot whales back out towards the sea. Secondly, he needed to turnaround the rest of the whales heading towards him. Finally, he needed to save London from flooding.

"Cumbakeer?" Said George, staring along the River, "I think we're going to need a faster boat."

George thought fast and made a plan, "Porter, can you tell the whales to follow the sound of our engine back out towards the sea", "Woof" barked the terrier.

"Cumbakeer, I need you to fly straight back to the Tower and tell the Ravenmaster what you told me, especially about the wave and the flooding. Tell him I'm going to head for the whales but I can't stop a flood."

"Squawk, Cumbakeer Withme sandwich will get the message through," he announced importantly, "I'm a Royal Raven you know". He took off into the darkness.

George started the engine and began to lead the whales back down the river. The tide was now flowing back this way but progress felt painfully slow, they were never going to get there at this rate. As they approached Blackfriers Bridge, George absentmindedly reached into his pocket and felt the ball of twine he had stuffed in his pocket a few long hours ago. He looked at the gulls, "Blackfriar, how many friends have you got?" Without hesitation, the gull called loudly into the air and they were almost immediately joined by a dozen more, "How many do you need?"

CHAPTER 9

The Whales

Cumbakeer watched the Ravenmaster as he relayed the news over the special red telephone that gave him a direct line to the Queens bedroom. When he finished, he paused to listen. "Yes Ma'am. Will do Ma'am. I'll have the kettle on when you get here". He put the phone down and looked at Cumbakeer who had now been joined by some of the other Ravens. "Right, the Queens on er way and she's bringing the Mayor, the Prime Minister and the Head of the Army with her so you lot better be on yer best behaviour."

A few minutes later, black cars started to arrive at the Tower, driven at high speed behind police cars with their blue flashing lights. The Ravenmaster, still in his vest but with his Hat on Saluted smartly as the Queen was helped out of a large black Range Rover by a footman who was sporting a pair of West Ham Pyjamas. The Queen wore a dressing gown and slippers but had managed to swap her hair rollers for an emergency Tiara that she kept in her handbag for just this sort of occasion. Next to arrive was the Prime Minister, followed by the Mayor and the Head of the Army, all of whom were also dressed in PJ's and looked like they had just woken up, which of course they had.

"May I suggest we head to the roof" said the Queen, who was always good in a crises. From the roof of the Tower, the party had a perfect view of the Thames. That's how it came to pass that the Queen, The Prime Minister, The Mayor of London and The Head of the Army were all watching as George and Porter raced along the river Thames in their boat at high speed being towed behind a pack of 50 seagulls, each holding a length of garden twine in its beak.

Porter lay down low as the boat skipped over the surface of the water as fast as a galloping horse. George had a wide smile on his face as the wind rushed through his hair and splashes of water sprayed over the bow of the boat, not only had his plan worked brilliantly, but this was even better than a roller coaster. He watched as the sprawling streak of gulls in front of them flew low to clear under Tower bridge and then accelerated again, as they emerged from the other side. At this rate, they were going to get to the approaching whales in no time at all. But the smile dropped from Georges face as he remembered the approaching flood. By now, the news would have reached the Ravenmaster but there was no way he could evacuate London in time. George then wondered if his boat would manage to stay afloat when the wave came through and he tightened the straps of his life jacket a little more.

As they came around a bend in the river, Blackfriar, who had been scouting ahead, circled back and descended low to fly directly over George. "I can see em, about half a mile ahead". He then climbed up in front of the Gulls to lead them on the the right spot. George looked ahead, squinting his eyes through the spray of water. There in the distance were puffs of water being shot into the air that he now recognised as the whales clearing their blow holes. First, he saw just one or two, then as they got closer, there seemed to be 10, 20, 50 of them, stretching off into the darkness.

"Porter, I hope they listen to you, there's so many of them!"

said George as the Gulls, lead by Blackfriar slowed down as they approached the lead whale.

Porter Gave a low rumbling growl, he had a determined look on his face and with final glance at George, where he seemed to waggle his eye brows as if to say, 'wish me luck', he leapt into the murky dark water.

It was no good. The normally calm and placid whales were all shouting and and making a racket under the water as a mild panic lead them still further along the river. George saw Porters head poke up out of the river several times, barking at Blackfriar who translated to George. "He can't make em listen. They're arguing amongst themselves."

George felt helpless and frustrated as he watched Porters desperate efforts to convince the whales to turn back fail. He had to do something and fast, he looked around him, desperate for something that might help Porter. Then, it struck him, hadn't the Ravenmaster said that whales hated the sound of the engine? He climbed over the oars to the back of the boat and pulled the starter, it rumbled and spluttered to life and he began to drive the boat in a large curve, shepherding the front of the whale pod away. There were a hundred whales or more and one was several times bigger than George's little boat. George knew that at any time, contact with one of these immensely powerful creatures could tip the boat over and if that happened, all hope would be lost. He concentrated on keeping close enough to the whales to drive them back, but not so close at to risk capsize. On the third sweep across the river, he scooped up Porter, who was glad to be back in the boat after swimming in the cold amongst the pack of panicking whales. Georges plan was working, albeit slowly. He has managed to stop them from swimming further along the river and was gradually pushing them back.

George looked admiringly at his dog. It was one thing to drive a little boat around amongst the mass of giant creatures, but his brave little dog had been swimming around in the middle of them. "That took some guts Porter", Porter, looking wet and tired wagged his tail.

CHAPTER 10

Ravens to the Rescue

Back on the Roof of the Tower, a communications centre had been set up. Various people in had arrived and were busy plugging in equipment. Radio sets and field telephones were being hastily put out on tables. The Ravenmaster handed a cup of tea to the Queen in a chipped novelty cup that said, 'Keep calm and drink tea' on it.

"Thank you Ravenmaster, have you heard any more news from the Ravens?" She enquired. Not yet your Majesty, but I've got my best birds on it.

Cumbakeer and Geroff (who's full name was Geroff Mylunch) were already flying out across the Thames with strict instructions from Buster to fly directly back to the boat and assist George and Porter in anyway possible. They beat their wings with a sense of purpose, proud to be given an important role in the unfolding events. As they flew high along the river, Cumbakeer noticed a Milk Lorry, starting it's early morning delivery of fresh milk. "Eer, Geroff, look at that!" Geroff followed Cumbakeers gaze along a line of terraced houses and there sparkling under the street lights was a line of milk bottles, one on each doorstep. "We can't" Said Geroff firmly, though his wing beats had already slowed down as he said this. "I mean, we've got to save London."

"O course we can't!" said Cumbakeer in agreement, "We is Royal Ravens on a mission. It would be a wosname, depiction of duty. Hang on, is that a pint of cream?"

"Cream?" Exclaimed Geroff, "you're right, and I bet some of those milk bottles is full fat!"

"Full fat.." repeated Cumbakeer his eyes glazing over.

Back at the Tower, The Head of the Army, still wearing his action man Pyjamas, was showing the Queen and the Prime Minster a machine called a seismometer. "It records even the smallest of earthquakes" he said proudly. "We had it rushed here from the Geology department at the University of London.". The Queen looked at it with interest, "and how does it work?" She enquired. The Head of the Army stared at the machine. "We're not quite sure your Majesty" he said eventually, "Then perhaps you should also fetch the Geology professor?" "Good idea Ma'am", the general turned and shouted some orders at the men behind him.

The Queen sipped her tea and looked around her. The Prime Minster and the Mayor were busy giving detailed instructions to their assistants to arrange emergency makeup, wardrobe and a TV crew.

"Buster" she said quietly, "No one seems to be actually doing anything."

"No." Agreed the Ravenmaster, "lets hope young George comes up with something".

Just then, the Tower began to shake.

CHAPTER 11

Tsumami

"What's that?" Said Cumbakeer lazily, pulling his beak from the top off a milk bottle, cream splattered across his feathers. "Woss what?" hiccuped Geroff who was busy picking the top off of a third bottle of milk. "Felt like the whole ground moved?" "Nah", said Geroff who gave up on his bottle and lumbered unsteady across to Cumbakeer, "you're always like that when you've hit the cream too hard. Gis a bit of yours will ya?" Cumbakeer stood swaying unsteadily on his feet as Geroff poked his head into the bottle and came out again, milk completely covering his beak and face, Geroff belched. "Now. What was it we was supposed to be doing?" "Ss s saving London" hiccuped Cumbakeer. "Thas it! Saving London!" Exclaimed Geroff who promptly fell flat on his back and began to snore.

The first George and Porter knew about the earth quake was the sound of car alarms going off on the river bank. The water rippled and they could see slates falling from the roofs of riverside warehouses into the water.

"There is it!" Shouted George above the din of the engine. "How long do we have before the wave hits us?"

"Depends how fast it's moving and how far out it is, I'll send some of my gulls ahead and see if they can spot it coming". A troop of Gulls set of towards the horizon that now had the slightest hint of dawn light creeping into it.

George continued to drive the whales back and soon he could see a line of large concrete and metal structures spanning the river.

George studied them as they materialised out of the fog and a smile broke out across his face "Porter, that there is The Thames Barrier!" He shouted. "I've seen all about this on TV, it's a flood defence! They can raise a barrier right across the River, if we can raise the Thames Barrier in time, it might just be enough to stop to the flood. He turned to the black headed Gull, "Blackfrier, we need to get a message back to the Ravenmaster, ask them to raise the Thames barrier as soon as possible!" Blackfriar picked two of his fasted gulls to rush this message back to the Tower and George focussed his efforts back onto the whales, if he could just shepherd them through the barrier before it closed then all might still be well.

The roof of the Tower was now a hive of activity. The Head of the Police, London life boat, coast guard, Fire service and ambulance service had all now arrived and set up their own HQ. They were busy delegating tasks to each other, each commander keen to ensure that they could blame someone else if it went wrong. Army, Police and TV Helicopters were beginning to buzz overhead and someone was even handing out high visibility vests.

The Queen looked on over this scene with bemusement when a Gull landed on the Battlement and whispered his urgent message to the Ravenmaster. "Of course!" Shouted Buster, "can't believe I didn't think of it myself, your Majesty, you must order the closing of the Thames Barrier!"

CHAPTER 12

Repaid in Kind

An argument was in full swing on the roof of the Tower as to whose job it was to close the barrier and the correct procedure for an emergency closing of the barrier. The lady who had been handing out the luminous vests was insistent that a full health and safety assessment was required before they could even think of shutting it, someone else from the Coast Guard was doubtful as to whether it would work and a man who had somehow managed to put a suit jacket and tie on over his pyjamas was asking which department was going to pay the bill for the closure. The Prime Minster was busy working on his speech for the morning news and said he didn't want to interfere until they had run a focus group to work out if shutting the barrier was popular with voters.

Buster pulled the unlit pipe from his beard, "By the time this lot get their act together, it will be too late". He called a Raven across to him, "Buzzoff" he said, "Go back to George with this Gull here and tell him that we probably wont be able to close the barrier in time. He needs to save himself and Porter now, tell him to save themselves." Buzzoff memorised the message and set off with the

Gull.

A few minutes later, Buzzoff (full name Buzzoff Wilya) and the Gull had relayed Busters message, the news was devastating to George. They were so close, and now he was to abandon the mission? Porter Barked loudly, Buzzoff, Blackfrier and the other birds listened intently.

"Right' said Blackfriar as he grasped what Porter wanted. "Ees mad. He wants to get the whales to shut the barrier. But we ain't got long. See my Gulls are coming back already, the wave can't be far off. George looked up and sure enough he could see the gulls blackfrier had dispached returning back along the river silhouetted by the early morning light. George killed the engine and Porter, for the third time that night, dived into the water and swam towards the huge expanse of whales.

Now the earth quake had passed, the whales were much calmer. It took some time to settle them down but assisted by the large female he had rescued earlier that night and using his best whale voice, Porter finally managed to make himself heard. It's difficult to translate precisely what Porter said because whale language is very different to that of Humans and it takes a very long time to say each word but Porter patiently explained what he wanted them to do. After he had finished, the whales swam into a huddle to discuss Porters request. The leader then approached Porter. "You have risked much to save us today. We will do what we can in turn to help you".

Back on the surface, Blackfriers Gulls had now landed back on the boat. "7 maybe 10 minutes at most" they said solemnly. George looked at the water, whale humps now visible for hundreds of meters through the thinning mist of the morning sky. "Come on Porter, we've got to get out of here" he said to himself through gritted teeth.

As he watched the whales began to arrange themselves, first in a large circle and then a line as each one peeled off to take his place on the barrier. Soon George could see a line of whales stretching across the full width of the river patiently swishing their tales in the water. There were at least 100, too many to count. He then heard a loud trumpet like groan from one of the whales and on that signal, they dived together as one, using their combined strength to drive the enormous metal barrier into place.

Porter swam back to the boat, as George pulled him back aboard, he could see a large wall of water coming towards them, building in height as it closed in on them along the river. The barrier was already half way up now but the water was closing in fast. Porter and George stared, frozen in terror, their hearts racing. The barrier inched up with the enoumous combined strength of the whales but it seemd to George that the wave must reach them first. George gripped the seat of the boat with one hand and a handful of Porters fur with the other, he resolved to hold onto both with all his strengh if the boat went over. Everything then seemed to happen in slow motion, the wave was now towering above them, white foam dripping from the top of it's leading edge. George's heart sank as he realised they were too late but the whales must have sensed how close the wave was because all of a sudden, with a last heave of effort the barrier rose several metres in one swift movement, there was a loud clanging noise as it locked in place just a few seconds before the wave arrived. As the torrent of water hit the barrier it burst high into the air, spraying foam and a few unlucky fish over the top as the tremendous energy of the wave was absorbed and rebounded by the great Thames Barrier.

As the water receded, the whales, happy that they had now repaid kind with kind, made their way back to the North Sea with the rebounding wave, signalling thanks and kind words to Porter as they went.

CHAPTER 13

Loyal Order of Keepers

George and Porter stared at each other in silence for a full minute. "Right" Said George finally, looking at his watch, is was 5.15am, "lets get back to the Tower, we are supposed to be home by sunrise".

They sat in silence as the little engine chugged along, it had been a close run thing. By the time George steered his little boat back into traitors gate, he could see television crews beginning to arrive. Buster, flanked by his Ravens met the boat as George cut the engine. "Are you two in one piece" he enquired with a broad grin across his face. George looked at Porter and nodded, "I think so" was all he could manage. He wanted to explain what had happened but before he could get his thoughts in order Buster said, "Don't say anything else now, the birds have already told me what you two did, impressive work lads, but we've got to get you away from here before one of these TV crews notices you". He lead Porter and George back to the Tower, choosing a route that kept them all out of sight of the press and cameras. They went along two stone passage ways, up and down some very old stone steps and across an area of open grass towards a large wall. Buster lead them to a small door which was almost entirely overgrown with ivy. It was still dark and mist lingered in the air so George couldn't be certain but he thought they must now be on the far side of the Tower. Buster swept the Ivy aside and pulled a very large iron key from his belt. He unlocked the door which creaked as it swung open. "This way then" said Buster over his shoulder. They followed the Raven Master up some very steep stone steps and onto a small hallway, at the end of the hall was a very large heavy looking wooden door. "There's someone who wants to meet you" he smiled. Porter trotted ahead and sat expectently at the door his tail thumping against the floor. George pushed gently against the door which opened with surprising ease, inside was a stone walled chamber, about the size of a large school classroom but with a high ceiling made of thick wooden beams. On the walls were various paintings and some tapestries depicting birds. A fire was roaring in the large fireplace and either side were two large wingback chairs. Sitting in one of the chairs, still in her dressing gown and slippers was The Queen. "Do come and sit down, you must be very tired". George, who in a state of shock and wondering how many more surprises there were to come, sat down. Porter, Goerge noticed, seemed quite at home, he wagged his tail and made a bee line for the queen, putting his head on her lap as she ruffled his ears. The Queen then put her hand into her handbag and pulled out a dog biscuit which she gave to Porter before ushering him into a dog bed by the fire. The Queen turned to George, "I'm awfully sorry, I'm afraid I don't have any biscuits for us I'm afraid". George suddenly remembered his Dads hotel biscuits in his pocket, "Oh, I think I might have some" he pulled the bisuits out of his pocket, spilling the last of the twine onto the floor. The Queen looked at the squashed and battered packet with delight, "Caramel Short Breads, my favourite!".

The Queen listened carefully as George recounted the story of the evening, interrupting only twice, once to make sure George had another biscuit and the second time to remark how clever he had been to use the birds to pull his boat along so quickly. When he had finished, the Queen sat in thoughtful contemplation. George looked around the walls as she did so and noticed the paintings were all of Men and Women with Dogs. One of the paintings had a Dog in it that looked just like Porter. "I see you are admiring some of our paintings" remarked the Queen, "as you can see, both you and Porter come from a long line of Rescue Dogs and Keepers. This one here" she gestured "is Porters great great great grandfather" George peered at the plaque at the bottom of the frame, 'Charles Darwin and Beagle', "Charles Darwin?" Exclaimed George. "Indeed", said the Queen, "that was one of our most successful partnerships".

"I'm sure one day your picture too will hang on this wall George" added the Ravenmaster who then turned to the Queen, "Ma'am, time is short if George and Porter here are to make it home before they are reported missing". The Queen straightened up in her Chair "Indeed", as she fumbled in her Handbag the Ravenmaster turned back to George. "Now young George, as you can see from the paintings on the walls here, the Order of Keepers goes back a very long way" George looked around and saw one of the pictures had a woman in a chariot with what looked like Roman Soldiers in it and he wondered just how old "but whilst you will always have the gratitude of your Queen and the knowledge that you saved a lot of lives, I'm afraid no one else can know what you did here tonight." He paused. "Apart from anything else, everyone would think you were stalk raving bonkers. The worlds not ready to know about us yet." George let this sink in. He was right of course. Even his best friend Harry would think he was lying through his teeth if he told him about half the events of the evening. "Now, George, stand up" George stood up and Porter came and sat faithfully at his feet. The Queen stood, cleared her throat and said, "I hearby admit you to the Loyal Order of Keepers", as she did so, she pinned an impressive medal onto George's chest.

Buster lead them back along a hidden walkway on top of a wall above a wide grassy area, George could hear the prime minster speaking to the Cameras on the other side of the wall saying "Indeed when I heard the news of impending doom, I at once ordered the Thames Barrier to be shut and thanks to me, disaster has been averted". Buster Laughed. "Course you did, muppet" he said and George laughed, "at least we know who the real hero is" he winked at George.

Suddenly there was a flap and two thumps as one Raven missed the top of the wall next to Buster and fell onto the floor and another tried to land too fast and skidded across the stone flagstones and slammed into the wall. "I was wondering what happened to you two!" Exclaimed the Ravenmaster as Cumbakeer and Geroff picked themselves up and waddled towards him unsteadily. He looked at the white stains on their breast feathers, "You two have been at the cream again haven't you? I dunno, when will you lot learn"

He turned back to George, "Now, what time is it?"

"6.42am" said George. "Great, you still have about 10 minutes before sunrise. Now, I've got to leave you here, it's the rules. I don't know how you get here and I don't know how you leave. But remember, if you ever need me, just send a message with the birds. Now," he said looking down pitifully at Geroff and Cumbakeer, "I'd better go and deal with these two Jokers" With that, he turned on his heel and walked away.

Porter barked happily at George and trotted on ahead, George followed him back through the maize of walkways and turrets, back through the hidden door to the treehouse, across his garden and finally, to bed.

It was nearly 11am before George's Mum finally woke him up. "You looked so peaceful I didn't like to disturb you" said Mum as George yawned. George rubbed his eyes, Porter was sound asleep under the window in his room.

A dream? Thought George. Surely, it was a dream, he shut his eyes again and tried to doze off. As he lay in bed he could hear the radio blaring up from the kitchen downstairs.

"..thankfully no-one was injured in the earthquake and a flood was miraculously averted.." George opened his eyes.. could it have really happened? There on the table next to his bed was the medal, he picked it up, 'Loyal Order of Keepers'. He got out of bed, turning the medal over and over in his hands, it looked like a sort of flower. He looked at Porter sleeping soundly, put the medal on the shelf by his bed and headed downstairs for breakfast.

BOOKS IN THIS SERIES

Porter

Porter the Rescue Dog is the first in a series of adventures, if you have enjoyed this book then join our mailing list, or follow us on social media and youtube for more!

Search online for Porter the Rescue Dog.

Porter In Central America

The sudden appearance of an exotic looking bird on the roof of Plumb Tree Cottage could mean only one thing, an animal was in trouble and based on the bright colours of the birds plumage, George could tell this was going to take him far away from home.

As the scale of the situation emerges, it's clear that George and Porter are going to need a lot of nerve, a lot of help and a large slice of luck to pull this rescue off!

Printed in Great Britain
by Amazon

18685632R00034